This book belongs to

....

This is the story of a man called Joe,

and what happened in his shoe shop, long ago.

Ready to start? Away we go!

There's something else,

can you guess what?

Throughout this book there's

a slipper to spot.

The Elves
and the
Shoemaker

Illustrations by Sara Baker

make
believe
ideas

Old Joe is a shoemaker.
He does not sell many shoes.

Old Joe is very poor.

Joe *is* tired and hungry.

"There *is* nothing to eat!"
says *his* wife, Flo.

Joe has one piece of leather.
He leaves it on the table.
"I will make the shoes
tomorrow," he says.

The next morning, Flo goes into the shop.

"Look at these new shoes!"
Flo calls to Joe.

11

A lady buys the shoes.
She pays lots of money.

Joe buys more leather.
He leaves it on the table.
"Will it happen again?"
he asks himself.

The next day, there are
two new pairs of boots
in the shop.

Joe and Flo sell the boots.
They make lots of money.

Every night, Joe cuts
some leather.

Every morning,
he finds new shoes.

On Christmas Eve,
Flo says, "Let's find
out who helps us."

18

At midnight, Flo and Joe
see two small elves.
They are in their
underwear!

"It's cold!" says Joe.
"We will make them
clothes!" says Flo.

Joe and Flo make clothes
for the elves. They leave
the clothes on the table.

The elves find the clothes.
They put them on.

"This is our pay!" they say.
"Now we can be on our way!"

The elves leave the shoe shop.

They wave
good-bye to Joe and Flo.

Ready to tell

Oh no! Some of the pictures from this story have gotten mixed up! Can you retell the story and point to each picture in the correct order?

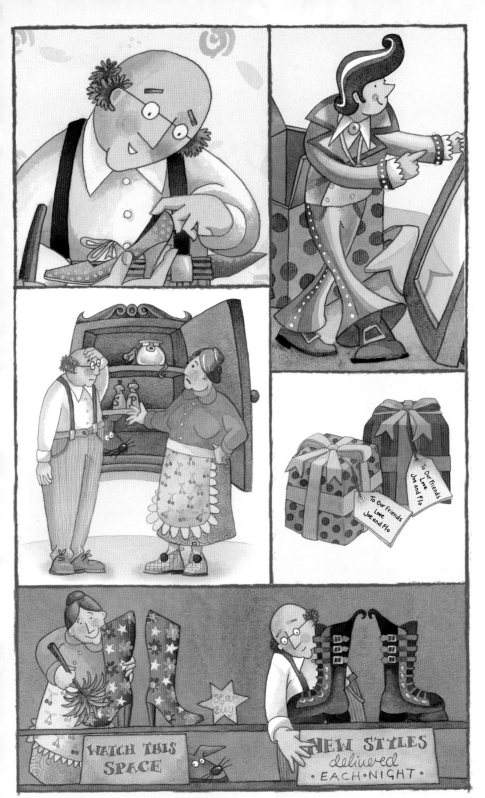

27

Picture dictionary

Encourage your child to read these words from the story and gradually develop their basic vocabulary.

boot

clothes

elves

lady

leather

shoemaker

shoes

shoe shop

wife

Key words

Here are some key words used in context. Help your child to use other words from the border in simple sentences.

Joe **is** a shoemaker.

The elves work **all** night.

They make new shoes.

Joe **and** Flo are happy.

The elves **go** away.

Make some special shoes

Here's an easy way to make your own pair of very special shoes – just like those from Joe and Flo's shop.

You will need

• a pair of canvas shoes (ask Mom or Dad if you can decorate them) • decoration materials: e.g. fabric paint, gold and silver marker pens, glitter paint • masking tape

What to do

1 Wash the shoes well, and leave them to dry completely.
2 While the shoes are drying, think about how you want to decorate them and get together everything you need. Let your imagination go wild! Bright colors work well on white canvas shoes, but black sneakers look great with silver, gold, or glitter paint.
3 When the shoes are dry, put them on a table covered with newspaper and get to work. Follow any instructions on the packaging. You may need to be patient and wait for one color to dry before you add another.
4 If you prefer neat patterns, use masking tape to help you make straight lines or neat blocks of color. (Ask a grown-up to help you.)
5 When you have finished, leave the shoes to dry. No one else will have a pair of shoes quite like these!